# For Luca

# I'll do it, Granny

By Dawn May

Illustrations by Phil Goss

1804630009

ISBN: 978-1-910385-01-2

Jake's granny has Parkinson's.
So Jake gets to help out a lot.

Granny likes to bake cakes.

Jake helps her ...

... to get everything ready.

Jake and Granny mix it all up ...

... and then they wait for it to cook.

What a lot of washing up!

But Jake gets to help out with
the eating, too.

Granny's garden needs
a bit of working on.

Are you all right up
there, Granny?

Lovely, dear. What's going on down there?

Granny has a dog,
Spike, and he keeps
on getting out.

So Granny and Jake get
to work on the hole.

Jake helps Granny with the shopping.
This is fun!

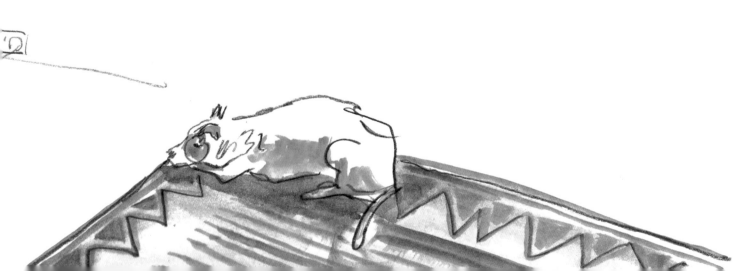

Thank you, Jake. I love it when we do things together.

# Coming Soon

Steady on, Granny

Cheer up, Granny

Can we talk about it?